Power Up, PJ Masks!

Based on the episode
"PJ Power Up!"

Ready-to-Read

Simon Spotlight
New York London Toronto Sydney New Delhi

SIMON SPOTLIGHT
An imprint of Simon & Schuster Children's Publishing Division
1230 Avenue of the Americas, New York, New York 10020
This Simon Spotlight edition December 2018
Adapted by Delphine Finnegan from the series PJ Masks
All rights reserved, including the right of reproduction in whole or in part in any form.
SIMON SPOTLIGHT, READY-TO-READ, and colophon are registered trademarks of
Simon & Schuster, Inc.
For information about special discounts for bulk purchases, please contact Simon &
Schuster Special Sales at 1-866-506-1949 or business@simonandschuster.com.
Manufactured in the United States of America 1118 LAK
10 9 8 7 6 5 4 3 2 1
ISBN 978-1-5344-3080-8 (hc)
ISBN 978-1-5344-3079-2 (pbk)
ISBN 978-1-5344-3081-5 (eBook)

Connor, Greg, and Amaya
like PJ Robot.

Greg pretends to be a robot.

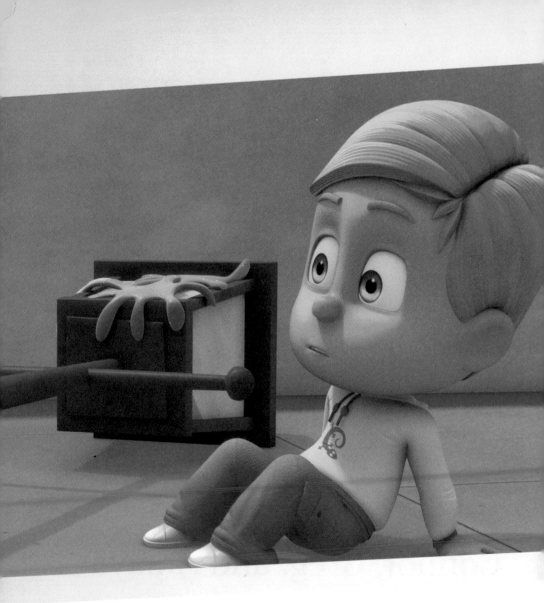

He slips on a Sticky Splat.

Night Ninja must be
up to something.
This is a job
for the PJ Masks!

Amaya becomes Owlette!

Greg becomes

Gekko!

Connor becomes Catboy!

They are
the PJ Masks!

PJ Robot

wants to help.

He looks

at the Picture Player.

He upgrades the walkie.

Now it shows videos.

The PJ Masks head out.
But PJ Robot

must stay behind.

PJ Robot presses buttons on the Picture Player.

Then the room goes dark.

A crystal appears!

Night Ninja

and the Ninjalinos

practice their powers.

They lift buildings.
Soon they can take
any building they want!

The PJ Masks

leap into action.

PJ Robot calls Owlette.
The crystal is blasting
strange beams.

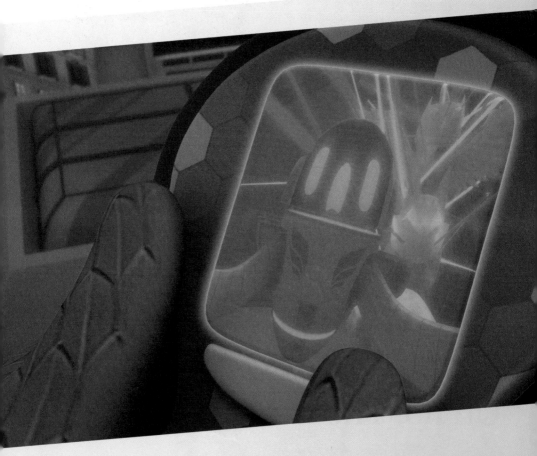

Oh no! The three heroes
have lost their powers!

They race to PJ Robot and

Headquarters.

PJ Robot tries to power up Headquarters. He becomes low on energy.

The PJ Masks know

he was just trying to help.

They feel the energy
from the crystal.

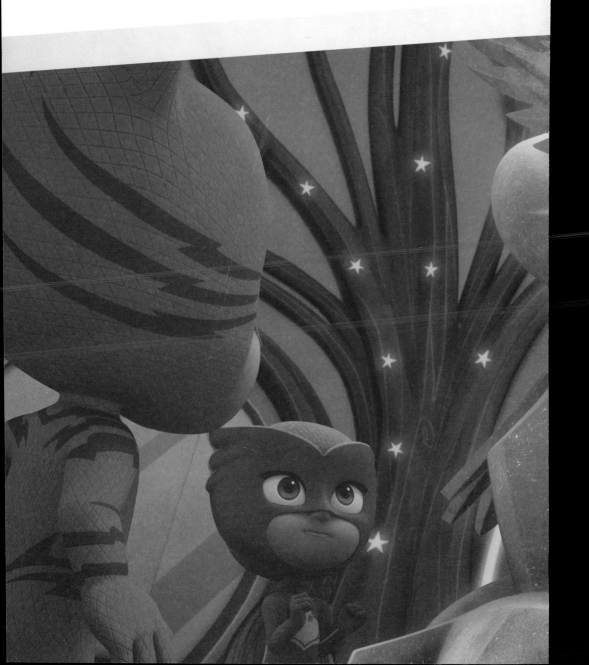

They transform and
are stronger than ever.

Catboy is even faster
with his Super Cat Stripes.

He traps the Ninjalinos
so they cannot move.

Gekko has

Super Gekko Shields.

They block everything.

He sends Sticky Splats

back at the Ninjalinos!

Owlette has

Super Owl Feathers.

They make a strong barrier.

She stops the Ninjalinos
in their tracks.

"The crystal gave us
new powers! Thank you,
PJ Robot!" Catboy says.
The four heroes
celebrate together!